One Little Bird

For Mum and Dad, thank you for encouraging
me to follow my dream x — H.S

For P, S, B, J and K, love you all! x
And for animals everywhere. — S.W.

OXFORD
UNIVERSITY PRESS

Great Clarendon Street, Oxford OX2 6DP

Oxford University Press is a department of the University of Oxford.
It furthers the University's objective of excellence in research, scholarship,
and education by publishing worldwide. Oxford is a registered trade mark of
Oxford University Press in the UK and in certain other countries

Database right Oxford University Press (maker)

First published 2021

British Library Cataloguing in Publication Data available

ISBN: 978-0-19-277366-1

1 3 5 7 9 10 8 6 4 2

Printed in China

Paper used in the production of this book is a natural, recyclable product made
from wood grown in sustainable forests. The manufacturing process conforms
to the environmental regulations of the country of origin

One
Little
Bird

Sheryl Webster   Helen Shoesmith

OXFORD
UNIVERSITY PRESS

Rosa was one little bird
in a very tall tree.
She loved her nest.

It was cosy. It was comfy. And it was safe.

That was, until one day
the *awful* thing happened . . .

Rosa *swooped* and *dived*.

'Why are you taking away my tree?' she cried.

But the man waved her away.
'My lettuces won't grow in this shade,'
he said. 'You can find another tree.

You're *just* one little bird.'

Rosa didn't find another tree.
But she did find another home . . .

. . . at the top of the man's house!

'You've taken my home,
so I'm moving here,' she said.

No matter how many times the man shouted,

'Give back my hat!'
and 'You can't stay there!'

. . . Rosa
did
not
budge.

'Animals, everywhere!
We must stop people from
taking our homes!' she cried.

Rosa's words *swept* along streams,
flashed through forests, and *sailed* over oceans.

Soon, animals everywhere
were talking about one little bird.

So, when the tree fellers arrived
in the forest, and said . . .

'We need this wood to make things.
'You can find other trees!'

The animals remembered Rosa.
'If one little bird can stand up to them,
then so can we,' they all said.

And they wasted no time . . .

In a flash, the forest animals rushed into the tree fellers' houses.

The tree fellers didn't know what to do.
They *shouted*, they *shooed*, and they *chased*.

But the animals did not budge.

In other places, yet more *awful* things were happening . . .

People were clearing sloth's rainforest to farm crops.

They were digging up giraffe's
grassland to build a road.

And they were replacing monkey's
jungle with new houses.

But the animals in these
places remembered Rosa.

Before people knew it, they were finding . . .

. . . sloths on their sofas,

giraffes in their beds,

and monkeys in their bathtubs.

There were lions in their laundry,

and lemurs in their loos.

All over the world animals were
moving into people's homes . . .

. . . and they would not budge.

But soon people were getting angry
with the animals in their homes.

The animals were eating their food.
They were creating a mess.
The people wanted them gone!

This made the animals angrier too.
They had nowhere else to go!

When news of the trouble reached Rosa,
she knew something had to be done.

*There must be a way for people
and animals to live in peace, she thought.*

With no time to waste,
Rosa called animals and people
to an urgent meeting.

'It's time to work
things out!' she cried.

Once more Rosa's words
swept across land and sea.
Before long people and animals
gathered to listen to one little bird.

'What do you want?' Rosa asked the people.

'We want our homes back!' they said.
'We love our homes.'

'What do you want?' she asked the animals.

'We want our homes back!' they said.
'We love our homes too!'

And suddenly the people went quiet.

Rosa swooped down to speak with the people.

'Don't you remember, the world is our home too . . .

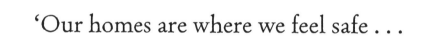

'Our homes are where we feel safe . . .

'They are where we find food . . .

and raise our young.
So please, will you try to think more about us?'

From that day, people
promised to take more care.

Although they still needed to grow crops
and build homes, they re-planted
wherever they could . . .

They recycled
and they re-housed.

It wasn't easy.
It wasn't perfect.
But it was a start . . .

And not very far away,
one little bird snuggled happily
into her new special spot.

And she did not budge.